Raymond Library

MONTVILLE

Books may be kept two weeks and may be renewed once for the same period except 7 day books and magazines.

A fine is charged for each day a book is not returned according to the above rule. No book will be issued to any person incurring such a fine until it has been paid. Five cents a day on two week books and magazines and ten cents a day on 7 day books.

Five books may be taken on a card, only one of which may be a 7 day book.
Three magazines per card.

All injuries to books beyond reasonable wear and all losses shall be made good to the satisfaction of the Librarian.

Each borrower is held responsible for all books drawn on his card and for all fines accruing cn the same.

Simon welcomes spring

Gilles Tibo

Tundra Books

My name is Simon and I love the spring.

When the winter snow begins to melt,
I go out with my drum to welcome spring.

I go to the garden to watch for flowers.

When the leaves come out of the earth
I tie on balloons to help them grow.

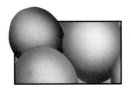

But the rains come down and wash them away.

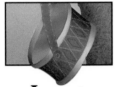

I go to a tree to ask the Owl:
"How can I make spring come?"

"Wait a while, Simon," said the Owl.
"When the birds come back from their winter home,
the trees will grow leaves and the flowers bloom."

I climb a hill to welcome the birds.
I build nests and Marlene brings houses.

I blow on my flute to call the birds.

But the birds fly by and do not see us.

I go to a field to ask a Rabbit.
"How can I wake the sleeping bears?
How can I tell them spring is here?"

"Wait a while, Simon," said the Rabbit.
"When the maple sap flows, the bears will wake."

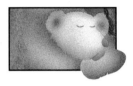

I go to the woods to get sap for the bears.

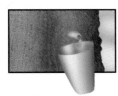

But the trees are in water
And I cannot reach them.

I sit alone and think to myself:

I could not make the flowers bloom
or the trees grow leaves
or the birds return
or the bears wake up.

I could not make spring come.

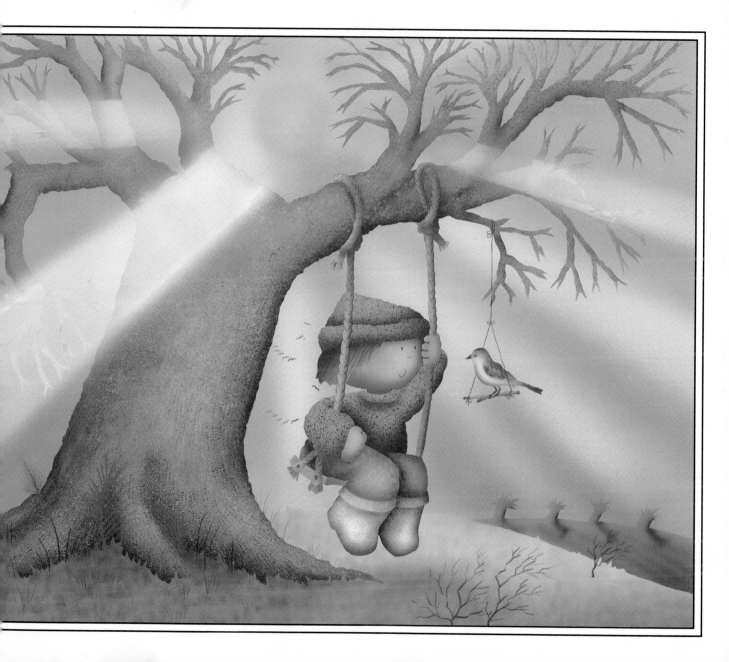

Then one day spring came by itself.
I went out with my friends to welcome it.

TO ANTOINE

© 1990, Gilles Tibo

Published in Canada by Tundra Books, Montreal, Quebec H3G 1R4

Published in the United States by Tundra Books of Northern New York, Plattsburgh, N.Y. 12901

Distributed in the United Kingdom by Ragged Bears Ltd., Andover, Hampshire SP11 9HX

Distributed in France by Le Colporteur Diffusion, 84100 Orange

ISBN 0-88776-247-6   Library of Congress Catalog Number: 90-70131

Also available in a French edition, Simon fête le printemps   ISBN 0-88776-248-4
Library of Congress Catalog Number: 90-70132

Canadian Cataloguing in Publication Data
Tibo, Gilles, 1951-

[Simon fête le printemps. English]
Simon welcomes spring

Translation of: Simon fête le printemps.
ISBN 0-88776-247-6

I. Title. II. Title: Simon fête le printemps. English.

PS8589.I26S5314 1990   jC843'.54   C90-090153-5   PZ7.T42Si 1990

The publisher has applied funds from its Canada Council block grant for 1990 toward the editing and production of this book.

Printed in Hong Kong by South China Printing Co. (1988) Ltd.